TOTALLY CRUSHED!

Adapted by Kiki Thorpe

Based on the series created by Terri Minsky

Disney PRESS

New York

Printed in the United States of America

First Edition
11 13 15 17 19 20 18 16 14 12

Library of Congress Catalog Card Number: 2002101336

ISBN 0-7868-4539-2
For more Disney Press fun, visit www.disneybooks.com

Lizzie McGuire

PART ONE

CHAPTER ONE

Yee-hah! It was hoedown time at Hillridge Junior High School. On Friday afternoon, the school gym echoed with the sound of dozens of pairs of sneakers squeaking on the varnished floor, as the eighth-grade physical education class practiced square dancing. As part of a special P. E. unit, the boys and girls were grouped together in order to learn how to dance. Today the gym instructor, Coach Kelly, had traded her usual high-tops for a pair of beat-up black cowboy boots. Now she stood in the center of the room, stomping in time to the fiddle music and calling out the square-dancing moves. All around her, eighth graders dressed in gym uniforms were trying to act as though they were having fun.

Lizzie swung on the elbow of a boy from her math class and glanced enviously across the square to the spot where her ex-friend, Kate Sanders, was dancing with Ethan Craft. Kate had tied the bottom of her T-shirt into a knot to show off her belly chain, and as she swung around Ethan, she grinned as if square dancing were her all-time favorite activity. Lizzie gritted her teeth. She'd had a crush on Ethan for ages, and it bugged her to see Kate having such a good time with him.

"Now, girls in the center with a right-hand star," Coach Kelly called out, clapping her meaty hands to the rhythm.

The girls moved into the center of the square and put their right hands together, walking around in a circle. Lizzie took the opportunity to complain to her friend Miranda.

"It's so unfair," Lizzie said with a pout. "How come Kate gets to dance with my potential boyfriend Ethan?"

"'Cause she *asked* him," Miranda replied. "You could have."

"Come on back and honor your partners," Coach Kelly barked.

"Yeah," Lizzie said to Miranda over her shoulder as the girls headed back to their dancing partners. "But then I'd have had to get up the nerve to talk to him."

"Come on back and honor your corners!" called Coach Kelly. The girls turned and curt- sied to the boys on their right. The boys bowed.

"Now allemande left!" shouted Coach Kelly. As Lizzie skipped around the edge of the square, she passed Kate, who was skipping in the opposite direction. Kate leaned in. "Howdy-do, Corner!" she said cheerily to Lizzie. "Guess what? Somebody has a crush on you. Oh, the things you learn in coed gym." Kate grinned and skipped away.

For a moment, Lizzie was suspicious. Kate wasn't usually very nice to her—why was she being so friendly now? On the other hand, Lizzie thought, who cares? Kate was in possession of some very important information.

Lizzie turned to Miranda, who was passing on her left. "Hey! Somebody's got a crush on me!" she exclaimed.

Miranda's eyes opened wide. "Who?" she asked excitedly.

"Give me a sec," Lizzie said. She turned back to Kate. The two girls circled around each other. "Name, please?" Lizzie asked.

"Oh, I can't tell you that," Kate protested.

"That would be gossiping. And that's wrong, Lizzie." Kate fluttered her eyelashes innocently, then gave Lizzie a wicked grin.

Lizzie sighed with exasperation. "She won't tell me," she told Miranda the next time they passed each other.

"All in the center with a right-hand star!" Coach Kelly commanded.

The whole square came together, and the dancers placed their right hands together.

"Well, maybe it's Quinn?" Miranda guessed as the group circled. "Boy most likely to play in the World Series."

"Quinn?" Lizzie pictured the tall, square-jawed star of the baseball team. She'd never been very interested in sports, but then again, she'd been meaning to pick up some new hobbies. "That's not so bad," she said, looking at Kate. But Kate shook her head "no."

"Left-hand star!" Coach Kelly called out.

The group reversed directions, putting their left hands together, and began to circle the other way. Gordo cut in behind Lizzie.

"I hear you have a gentleman caller," he told her.

"Whose name is . . . ?" Lizzie raised her eyebrows, waiting for the answer.

"I haven't heard," Gordo said. "Maybe it's Winston, the transfer from Mali."

A foreign student? She hadn't thought of that. "Ooh," Lizzie said. "Exotic."

"Yeah," Miranda agreed. "And he barely speaks English, so you don't have to worry about saying anything stupid."

Was it Winston who had the crush? Lizzie, Miranda, and Gordo all looked to Kate for the answer. But Kate smiled smugly and again shook her head "no."

"All around with a left-hand lady," Coach Kelly ordered.

The boys and girls "left-hand-ladied" around the circle, linking elbows as they passed from partner to partner. Suddenly, Lizzie realized that Ethan Craft was coming toward her down the square-dance chain! Her eyes opened wide. "Maybe it's . . . Ethan Craft?" she said with a gasp.

"That would be a crush return!" Miranda exclaimed.

Lizzie looked hopefully at Kate, who rolled her eyes. "In what universe, Lizzie McGuire?" she said snidely.

"Well, who then?" Miranda asked.

"Hi, Lizzie," a voice suddenly said behind her. Lizzie whirled around. There, standing before her in black socks, dorky sneakers, and tight gym shorts that showed way too much of his pale, skinny legs, was Larry Tudgeman. He beamed at Lizzie.

Lizzie glanced nervously over at Kate. Kate

smiled and put her hand over her heart, nodding her head "yes." She winked and gave Lizzie a sarcastic thumbs-up. Lizzie wanted to throttle her.

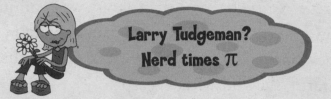

Larry Tudgeman?
Nerd times π

"Now, all in the center with a great big yell!" Coach Kelly cried.

Before the stunned Lizzie had a chance to think, the students rushed toward the center of their circles. "YEE-HAH!" they shouted, banging into her.

"*Ooof*," Lizzie grunted. She'd just been slammed. In more ways than one.

"Larry Tudgeman?!" Lizzie exclaimed after gym class, as she, Miranda, and Gordo walked down the hallway. "My first crusher! Oh, it's unfair!"

Miranda shook her head sympathetically. "My condolences."

"Tell me about it," Lizzie went on. "The guy hasn't changed his shirt since, like, the second grade." Larry Tudgeman had been wearing the same putty-colored polo shirt with a lime-green collar for as long as Lizzie had known him. Lizzie glanced down at her own hot pink T-shirt, flowered pants, and pink platform flip-flops. Fashion-wise, she and Larry were on different planets.

"Relax," Gordo told Lizzie. "It's just a crush. He's not going to do anything."

"That's true," Miranda agreed. "We've had a crush on Ethan Craft forever, and *we've* never done anything about it."

Lizzie tilted her head thoughtfully. "When you put it like that, it's not so bad. I guess you could say the crush has been crushed." She sighed with relief.

But she'd spoken a moment too soon. Suddenly, Larry Tudgeman popped out of the doorway of a nearby classroom and stepped right in front of Lizzie, blocking her path.

"Lizzie! There you are!" he exclaimed. He looked at Miranda and Gordo and lowered his voice. "Can . . . can I talk to you?"

Lizzie glanced at her friends, then followed Larry a few paces away, just out of their earshot.

"Uh, I . . . I was wondering," Larry hedged, "if, uh, maybe sometime you'd like to go out? Like on a date. This Sunday afternoon?" He looked at Lizzie hopefully.

"Um . . ." Lizzie gulped. What could she say?

Never! No way!
Not in a million years!
Nope! Nix! *Nyet!*

"Uh, I . . . I . . ." Now it was Lizzie's turn to stutter. "Well, I kinda have this . . . *thing*. So,

I can't," she lied. "Thanks for asking, though."

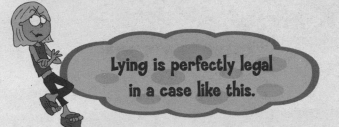

Lying is perfectly legal in a case like this.

Larry's face fell. "Oh, that's too bad," he said, looking down at the floor. He turned and shuffled down the hallway.

With a horrible sinking feeling, Lizzie watched him walk away. She'd narrowly avoided going on a date with Larry Tudgeman, the nerdiest guy in the world, so why did she feel so rotten now? Just then Miranda and Gordo walked up to her. They'd watched the whole scene. "So much for the crush being history," Lizzie told them unhappily.

"It's a good thing he has algebra next," Miranda said, looking down the hallway at Larry. "It'll cheer him up."

CHAPTER TWO

"Take that!" Mr. McGuire cried, pounding the video game controls with his thumbs. On the television screen in front of him, an enemy spaceship blew into bits. Mr. McGuire briefly raised one fist in victory, then began to hammer away at the controls again.

Seated on the couch next to his dad, Lizzie's ten-year-old brother, Matt, was working the other set of video game controls. His thumbs pumped furiously as he steered his spaceship around the screen, dodging enemy fire. The light from a series of onscreen explosions flickered across Mr. McGuire's and Matt's tense faces.

Crash! Suddenly, a huge clatter echoed through the house from the direction of the garage.

"Mom's home," Matt said, without looking up from the television.

A second later, the door opened with a bang, and Mrs. McGuire stormed into the living room. "Okay, that's it, guys," she growled.

"Hi, honey. Hard day?" Mr. McGuire asked cheerfully, continuing to watch the video game out of the corner of his eye.

"No," Mrs. McGuire snapped. "I had a wonderful day. Until I tried to park the car in the garage and couldn't. You know why?"

Matt nodded. "Because you turned your wheel too early, then panicked and turned it the other way really, really fast," he told her knowingly.

Mrs. McGuire stared at her son for a moment, then shook her head. "I don't know what you're talking about," she said quickly. "The reason I couldn't park is because the driveway is *filled* with your junk. The lawn is also filled with your junk. And where is that junk supposed to go?" She put her hands on her hips and waited. Mr. McGuire and Matt looked at each other and shrugged. "In the toolshed!" Mrs. McGuire exploded. "But it can't fit in the toolshed because the toolshed is so filled with your junk!"

"It's junk to you," said Matt. "But to us it's . . . stuff."

"Well, the stuff has got to go." Mrs. McGuire pursed her lips and gave her husband and son her best no-messing-around look. "Now!" she commanded.

"Party pooper." Mr. McGuire sulked.

"That's my job," Mrs. McGuire said brightly and marched off to make dinner.

A few moments later, Matt and his dad stood before the toolshed in the McGuires' backyard. Mr. McGuire pulled open the door, and a pile of "stuff," including cardboard boxes, tool kits, kites, baseball gloves, skis, skateboards, Boogie boards, and Rollerblades, tumbled out onto the lawn. A falling tennis racket whacked Mr. McGuire in the shin.

"Ow!" he cried, clutching his leg and hopping away.

Matt peered into the cluttered toolshed. "It's not messy," he insisted.

"Well, let's just move a few things around so it looks like we did something," Mr. McGuire suggested. They waded into their treasure trove and began to poke through all their old toys.

At the back of the shed, Matt moved aside a couple of cardboard boxes and discovered a kid-sized car made out of wooden crates and painted to look like an American flag. Matt roughly began hauling the car out of the shed.

"Hey, watch it," Mr. McGuire said.

"This can go," Matt said.

"That's my soapbox racer!" Mr. McGuire protested. He sighed admiringly. "What a beauty."

Matt looked at the dusty old car and curled his lip in disgust. "This thing?" he said. "*Lame-o.* Grandma-on-my-scooter goes faster."

"Hey!" Mr. McGuire said defensively. "You should have seen Grandma when she was in this thing." He thought for a moment and suddenly snapped his fingers. "Wait a second. Scooters are on their way out. We could shine this baby up, make it Y2K compatible, and voilà! We've got the Next Big Thing!" His eyes shone as he imagined himself rolling around in a pile of money he had made from selling soapbox racers. Matt looked at the racer with new respect. He climbed into the driver's seat and gripped the wheel, pretending to steer.

"Hey," Mr. McGuire said, snapping out of his reverie. "Get out of there. It's my turn."

Meanwhile, Lizzie was in the kitchen, helping her mother cook dinner. While Mrs. McGuire emptied canned tomatoes into a pot, Lizzie distractedly chopped a green pepper. All afternoon she'd been thinking about Larry Tudgeman. She still felt guilty about lying to him to get out of the date. But what else could she have done?

Lizzie leaned her elbows on the counter, watching her mother toss a pinch of oregano into the spaghetti sauce. "Mom, I . . . uh . . . need your advice," Lizzie said finally.

Her mom looked up in surprise. "Really?" she asked excitedly. "You want to talk to me?" Lizzie almost never wanted her mother's advice on anything.

"Um, yeah," Lizzie said, uncertainly.

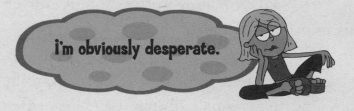

i'm obviously desperate.

"It's about a boy," she told her mother.

Mrs. McGuire's face lit up. "Aw, boy trouble. Oh, my God," she said, opening her arms to hug Lizzie. "Oh, honey, at last. Come here and tell me."

"No, no, no, no." Lizzie retreated, taken aback by her mother's dopey behavior. "Forget it," she said. She turned and headed for her room.

Mrs. McGuire reined in her enthusiasm.

"I'm sorry," she said, dropping her arms. She went back to the stove and began to stir the sauce again. "I really am. Now, really, tell me what it is," she said in a businesslike manner.

Lizzie heaved a sigh. "Okay. Well, what do you do if a guy you don't like—and never, ever will like—not in a *million* years"—she tapped her finger on the counter to emphasize her point—"what if he wants to go out with you?"

"Well . . ." Mrs. McGuire said carefully. "How do you know you don't like him if you haven't given him a chance?"

Lizzie wrinkled her nose. "You mean go out with him?"

Her mother nodded.

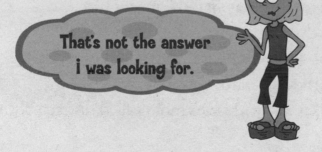

That's not the answer i was looking for.

Perhaps her mother didn't understand the seriousness of the situation. "Okay, let me rephrase the question, Mom." Lizzie tried again. "What do you do if the guy you don't like is a *total geek*?" She threw up her hands. "You have to agree with me in this case, Mom, I can't go out with him."

At that moment, Matt came running into the kitchen, his arms flapping frantically. "Mom! Mom! Emergency!" he cried. "Dad's stuck in his soapbox racer!"

"Okay! Okay!" Mrs. McGuire replied, but she wasn't really listening. She shook her head and turned back to Lizzie. "No," she said calmly, continuing their conversation, "in that case you may have to marry him, because that's the family curse."

"Jo! Honey! Help!" Mr. McGuire called from the backyard.

"Okay, okay," Lizzie's mom called distractedly,

while continuing to stir the spaghetti sauce. Matt waved his arms like an air traffic controller, trying to get his mother's attention, but Mrs. McGuire was still focused on Lizzie's problem.

"You mean, he could be my destiny?" Lizzie asked in horror. For a moment, she imagined their wedding day. There Lizzie would be, dressed in a gorgeous cap-sleeved wedding dress with a tulle skirt and a full-length veil, walking down the aisle with Larry Tudgeman, who would still be wearing his putty-colored polo shirt. Lizzie shuddered at the thought.

Mrs. McGuire shook her head. "I don't know," she answered. "But the one thing I do know about boys, honey, is that some of the best ones come in very strange packages."

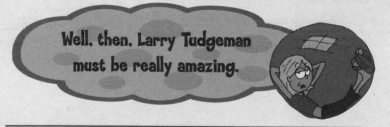

Well, then, Larry Tudgeman must be really amazing.

"I can't tell you what to do about the boy who likes you who you don't like. . . ." Mrs. McGuire said. "I'm just saying nobody likes to be rejected."

"I know." Lizzie sighed.

"Boys are very sensitive creatures," Mrs. McGuire went on, looking at her son. Matt, having failed in all his attempts to get his mother's attention, was now sitting on top of the counter, pretending to strangle himself. "Especially our kind," she added.

"Help!" Mr. McGuire cried again from the backyard.

"Oh!" Mrs. McGuire cried, suddenly realizing what was happening. "Your dad!" She put down the spoon and hurried out to the backyard to help her husband.

"*Thank you,*" Matt croaked, collapsing on the kitchen counter.

* * *

After dinner, Miranda and Gordo came over to Lizzie's house to hang out. The three friends sat together on the lawn furniture in Lizzie's backyard, sipping hot chocolate and discussing Lizzie's Larry problem. Lizzie tried to explain to her friends why she was considering going out with Larry Tudgeman.

"I wouldn't want Ethan Craft to blow me off the way I did Larry," she told them.

Gordo nodded. "Righteous thinking, Lizzie!" he said.

Miranda looked at him in amazement. "I was thinking the exact opposite, Gordo." She turned to Lizzie. "Have you lost your mind? Because you just *can't* go out with Larry Tudgeman."

"It's just one dumb date," Lizzie pointed out.

"One dumb date for Lizzie, but it's one *giant* date for every boy who has ever been dissed by a girl," Gordo declared. Lizzie and Miranda smiled. They knew Gordo wasn't exactly speaking from experience. He'd never even worked up the nerve to ask a girl out.

"So, she's a hero." Miranda shrugged and turned to Lizzie. "Suggestion: make sure Larry takes you someplace where no one will see you. Especially Kate."

"Miranda!" Lizzie scolded.

"Trust me," Miranda told her. "This could ruin your social status for, like, ever."

Lizzie slumped down in her chair, considering this.

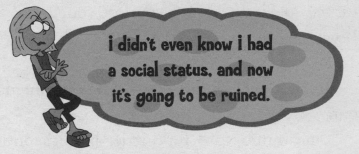

i didn't even know i had a social status, and now it's going to be ruined.

After Miranda and Gordo left, Lizzie went

into her kitchen and pulled out the telephone directory. She flipped to the *T*'s, and ran her finger down the page. Yep, there it was: "Tudgeman." The only one in the book. Lizzie chewed her lip, thinking about her options. Then she picked up the phone and dialed.

"Hello?" It was Larry. Lizzie cringed. She imagined him standing at home in a pair of dopey Spiderman pajamas. Or, she thought, maybe he sleeps in that polo shirt.

"Lizzie!" Larry said, just as she was about to hang up the phone. Lizzie froze. "I have Caller ID," he explained.

"Oh," Lizzie said awkwardly. "Great."

Sometimes i wish i lived in the Stone Age.

There was no backing out now. Lizzie took a deep breath. "I just wanted to know . . . if you're still available . . . for that date this weekend?" she managed to say.

For a brief second there was silence at the other end of the phone. Then Lizzie heard Larry yell, "Tudge rules! Tudge rules!" From the stomping noises in the background, she gathered he was jumping up and down.

"Okay," she said. "I guess that's a yes." Lizzie quickly hung up the phone.

"Hello?" Larry said, listening to the dial tone.

CHAPTER THREE

At 12:58 P.M. on Sunday afternoon, Lizzie was ready for her date with Larry Tudgeman. Dressed in green pants and an olive-colored cardigan that she hoped wouldn't clash too much with the lime-green collar of Larry's shirt, Lizzie sat on the couch, nervously chipping at her nail polish and wishing the date were already over. Her mother sat next to her, reading the newspaper. Every now and then she glanced over at Lizzie and smiled reassuringly.

Lizzie was so nervous that she practically jumped out of her chair when the doorbell rang. She looked at her watch. It was one o'clock sharp. Well, she thought, you could say one thing for Larry. He certainly was prompt.

Lizzie and Mrs. McGuire both stood up and walked to the door. "I can't believe I'm going to do this," Lizzie told her mother. "I'm gonna go out with Larry Tudgeman."

"And you're going to have a great time," Mrs. McGuire told her.

Lizzie gave her a pained smile and opened the door. Gordo walked into the house.

"What are *you* doing here?" Lizzie asked in surprise.

"I wanted to make sure that you were actually going to go through with this," he said.

"Good-bye!" Lizzie snapped, pointing to the door. But Gordo had already spotted Mr.

McGuire and Matt working on the soapbox racer in the backyard.

"Cool racer!" he exclaimed. He hurried though the house and out the back door to join them.

Ding-dong. Lizzie glanced at her mother and opened the door again. This time Larry was standing on the doorstep. He was holding a bunch of orange flowers and grinning at Lizzie. But . . . Lizzie's eyes opened wide with surprise. Instead of wearing his usual polo, Larry had on a black button-down shirt, and he'd combed his hair down over his pale forehead. He actually looked . . . cute!

"Larry?" Lizzie asked.

"You look handsome," Mrs. McGuire said.

"Oh," Larry said modestly. "I'm wearing my weekend shirt." He handed the bundle of flowers to Mrs. McGuire. "For you."

Mrs. McGuire beamed and held the

flowers to her nose to smell them. "Well, isn't that sweet?" she said, looking at Lizzie. Lizzie nodded and smiled.

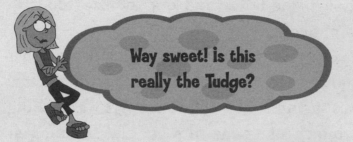

Way sweet! Is this really the Tudge?

"I had to battle alien forces in my garden to capture them for you," he told Lizzie's mom. Lizzie's smile faded.

Yep. It's the Tudge.

At that moment, Larry spotted the soapbox racer through the open back door. "Hey, cool racer!" he said, walking past Lizzie. She followed him to the backyard, where Mr. McGuire, Gordo, and Matt were huddled around the car. The ground around them was strewn with tools.

"Tudgeman," Gordo said in greeting when he saw Larry.

"Hey, kids, have a good time," Mr. McGuire said to Lizzie and Larry, leaning over to tighten a wheel with a wrench.

"Hold on one second there, Lizzie," Larry said. He walked over to the racer and pointed to a rear part of the car. "Dudes, if you remove the flanges there, you'll get maximum acceleration," he told the team.

Mr. McGuire and the boys stopped their work and looked at him in surprise. "Genius!" Matt said.

"All right, Tudge!" said Mr. McGuire, lifting his hand for a high five.

Larry kept his arms at his sides and shook

his head. "Oh, no," he said. "I don't want to get grease on my hands. I'm going out on a date." He gestured toward Lizzie and winked.

Mr. McGuire nodded. "Right," he said.

A half hour later, Lizzie and Larry were walking up to the entrance of the local science museum.

"You are gonna love this place!" Larry told her enthusiastically. "They have a Tesla coil!" Lizzie smiled halfheartedly.

Larry took Lizzie around to all his favorite exhibits. "This is a static electricity ball," Larry explained, leading Lizzie up to a giant silver orb. He touched the ball, and his short brown hair stood on end. "Now you try it," he said.

Lizzie placed her fingers on the ball. Her fingertips prickled. Out of the corner of her eye, Lizzie could see her long blond hair sticking straight up from her head. Larry started laughing. "You look like the Bride of Frankenstein," he said, then added, "I mean that as a compliment." Lizzie quickly took her fingers off the electricity ball and smoothed down her hair.

Lizzie and Larry played with radio waves, drove remote control cars, played keyboard with a humanlike robot, and created designs in a large display of magnetized metal shavings. When Lizzie glanced at her watch, she suddenly realized that more than two hours had passed and she hadn't even noticed. She was actually having fun!

"Isn't this the coolest place on earth?" Larry said as they looked at a display of colorful holograms.

"Yeah," Lizzie agreed—and she meant it!

* * *

Right before they left, Larry took Lizzie to his

favorite exhibit of all—a giant model of the human heart. Lizzie and Larry entered the heart through a blue tube meant to represent a pulmonary vein and stood in the center of the left atrium. The red walls around them pulsed, and Lizzie could hear a beating sound.

"See?" Larry explained, pointing around the room. "The heart looks nothing like a Valentine. It's actually the shape of an upside-down pear. Get this! In an average lifetime, the heart beats two and a half billion times."

"Wow," Lizzie said, looking at the gushing tubes around her. "Larry, you have all this knowledge and you explain yourself so well."

"I'm very intrigued about the world around me. Hey, look, Lizzie!" Larry's face suddenly lit up. "The mitral valve!" He grabbed Lizzie's hand and pulled her over to see a large, rubbery-looking flap in the wall.

"See, I like what I like," Larry told Lizzie,

after they'd finished inspecting the valve, "and I don't worry about what other people think. I mean, boy bands are a trend. But the circulatory system is forever."

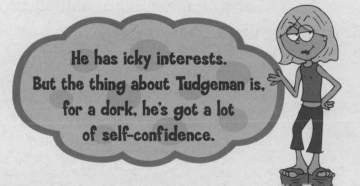

He has icky interests. But the thing about Tudgeman is, for a dork, he's got a lot of self-confidence.

Lizzie nodded. She had a whole new respect for Larry's take on the world.

Who's the dork? i freak if i wear the wrong shoes.

"Well," she said. "Thanks for a great day."

Larry smiled. Suddenly, the red lights inside the room started to flash. Sirens screamed, and the heart began to beat faster.

"Uh-oh," Larry said, looking around them. "I think he's having a heart attack!"

CHAPTER FOUR

"**W**hat do you mean you had a good time?" Miranda demanded the next day at school as she and Lizzie walked down the hallway. "You can barely stay awake through science class. You couldn't possibly have had fun at a whole museum about it."

"I said I had fun, okay?" Lizzie said impatiently. "It wasn't that bad. Larry's really nice, and I'm glad I went out with him."

Miranda rolled her eyes. "Whatever," she said.

"And there's a bonus!" Lizzie added. "The date earned me some karma points—to be redeemed with the boy of my choosing." She grinned at Miranda.

Miranda suddenly perked up. "You went out with Larry, so now you can go out with Ethan Craft!" she exclaimed.

"Or at least have the nerve to talk to him," Lizzie said. One thing at a time, she thought. She shouldn't get too carried away, but already Lizzie was imagining where she and Ethan would go on their first date—and she bet it wouldn't be a science museum.

Just then, Miranda and Lizzie spied Ethan standing only a few feet away at his locker. He was loading books into the messenger bag slung over his shoulder. Amazingly, none of his friends were nearby. Lizzie had a clear shot at him!

Miranda turned to her and grabbed her

arm. "Here's your opportunity," she said. "Ethan is close enough to make it look like a chance meeting, but not far enough to make it look like you've gone out of your way to bump into him." She smiled and slugged Lizzie on the shoulder. "Go get 'em, Tiger."

Lizzie took a deep breath. Then she set her sights and walked straight toward her crush. "Hey, Ethan," she said. Ethan turned around. Lizzie found herself looking right into his blue eyes. She opened her mouth to say something—

When, suddenly, Larry appeared from out of nowhere. "There you are, Lizzie!" he cried, putting his arm around her and steering her away from Ethan Craft. Lizzie glanced back over her shoulder and saw Ethan heading off down the hallway.

"Hey, Larry," she said flatly, trying to shrug his arm off her shoulders.

Larry didn't seem to notice that Lizzie was trying to squirm out of his grip. He looked at Lizzie, grinning from ear to ear. "I can't believe you're my *girlfriend*!" he said. "I'm the luckiest man alive!"

Lizzie's jaw dropped, and her eyes practically bugged out of her head. Larry's *girlfriend*? She looked at Larry in horror as he gave her shoulders a squeeze. Lizzie opened her mouth to say something, but no words came out.

"I am *not* Larry Tudgeman's girlfriend!" Lizzie insisted in an angry whisper later that morning. Lizzie, Miranda, and Gordo were huddled together at their lockers, discussing what Larry had said. Lizzie had spent the whole first half of the school day dodging Larry until she could figure out what to do.

Miranda was horrified. "Did you say something to make him think that you two are going out?" she asked.

Lizzie shrugged helplessly. "I told him he was nice."

"Well, there you go," Miranda said. "He's used to being blatantly rejected."

Lizzie hid behind her locker door, peering up and down the hallway to see if Larry were anywhere near. Gordo watched her and frowned.

"Look," he said. "You can't keep avoiding Larry forever. He's telling the whole school that you're his girlfriend." Lizzie groaned.

"Well, we've got to nip *that* in the bud," Miranda said curtly. "Deny, deny, deny," she advised Lizzie.

Gordo shook his head, still sympathizing

with Larry. "That's such a Kate move," he reprimanded Miranda. "That would only embarrass him in front of the whole school."

Miranda looked at him skeptically. As far as *she* was concerned, it was worth pulling a Kate move now and then to save one's reputation.

Suddenly, Lizzie had an idea. "What if I did the opposite of Kate? What if I went *out* with Larry? I mean, *pretended* to go out with him," she added hastily.

Gordo frowned, considering this. "Go on, McGuire," he said.

"Yes. Please explain," said Miranda.

"Okay, I'll fake 'go out' with him for a day, and then I can fake 'break up' with him."

"A clever plan," Gordo said, thoughtfully. "It completely eliminates the humiliation factor."

"But if anybody finds out, you're risking social destruction," Miranda warned.

"So, I'll take the risk," Lizzie told her. Miranda was starting to sound more and more like Kate, she thought, frowning. "I just don't want him to get hurt."

Miranda looked carefully at her. "You're not going to kiss him, are you?" she asked.

"Ew!" Lizzie squealed. "It'll be over way before then."

"But you guys have to keep this quiet," she added seriously. Gordo and Miranda crossed their hearts, promising not to say a word to anyone.

Just then the school's PA system crackled. "Today's announcements," Kate said, her perky voice echoing through the hallway. "Who's the school's hottest pair? Why none other than Tudge and McGuire. They're on fire!"

Lizzie glared at Miranda, who held up her hands innocently. "I didn't tell Kate anything!" she insisted.

"Ugh." Lizzie clutched her head.

The next few hours felt like the longest of Lizzie's life. Every time she turned around, Larry was standing next to her, grinning and trying to hold her hand. And whenever she least expected it, he would pop out of a class-room and give her a big bear hug. At break time, Larry pinned his *Star Wars* fan-club membership pin on the collar of Lizzie's jean jacket. In math class he wrote on the black-board:

$$\text{Lizzie + Larry} = \heartsuit^2$$

And at lunchtime he insisted on buying chocolate pudding for dessert. "One pudding, *two* spoons," he said, winking slyly at the lady behind the lunch counter and squeezing Lizzie's hand. He even paid a kid from the orchestra to serenade them at the lunch table!

Lizzie had to admit that all the attention was flattering. But going out with Larry, while trying to be sure that no one noticed, took a lot of energy!

Finally, it was time for gym. As Lizzie and Miranda filed into the gym from the girls' locker room, Lizzie saw Larry entering from the boys' locker room on the other side of the gym. Larry waved his arms at Lizzie. Lizzie raised her hand to her side and fluttered her fingers at Larry, smiling halfheartedly.

Miranda watched this interaction and snorted with disgust. "You know," she said to Lizzie. "If I didn't know better, I'd actually think that you and Larry *are* going out."

"Yeah, let's hope the breakup is as convincing," Lizzie said. "I don't want to lead him on any longer. This has been the longest day."

Tweeeeeeet! Coach Kelly's whistle pierced the stale, muggy air of the gym, and everyone snapped to attention. "Ballroom dancing," the coach barked. "Ladies, pick your partners."

Lizzie looked across the room to where handsome Ethan was leaning casually against a wall. Several girls rushed toward him, but Kate shoved through them and claimed him for her partner. Larry sidled over to Lizzie and took her hand.

Of all the days to be fake dating Larry.

Coach Kelly hit PLAY on a cassette recorder. As the music blared, Lizzie placed her hands on Larry's shoulders, and Larry put his hands on her waist. Awkwardly, they began to fox-trot around the gym. When Kate and Ethan danced by, Kate flashed Lizzie a sarcastic, "isn't that sweet?" grin. Lizzie rolled her eyes and looked away.

"One-two-three, one-two-three, one-two-three. . . !" Coach Kelly shouted, keeping time for the students.

"Ow!" cried Gordo, who was dancing with Miranda nearby. "You're stepping on my feet!"

"Well, you're completely off tempo," Miranda snapped back.

Lizzie decided that it was time to put her fake breakup with her fake boyfriend plan into action. "Hey, Larry," she said, as Larry steered her backward around the gym. "Meet me at the lunch patio after school, okay?"

Larry smiled smugly. "Can't get enough of me, huh?" he said.

"Um, right," Lizzie replied.

"We're the coolest couple here," Larry said, looking around the room. At that moment, he spotted Ethan suavely dipping Kate backward. Kate grinned as her long hair brushed against the floor. Ethan gracefully pulled her back up and twirled her around.

"Hey!" said Larry. "Let's do that." Before Lizzie could stop him, he grabbed her and tipped her backward. *Whoops!* Larry lost his grip and Lizzie tumbled to the floor. All the students stopped dancing and turned to look.

"Oh, I am so sorry, Princess," Larry said, leaning down to help her up.

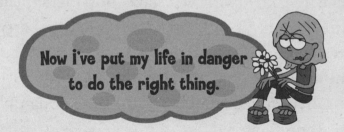

Now i've put my life in danger to do the right thing.

Lizzie sat up and rubbed her bruised knee. "Don't worry about it," she said casually. Grabbing the hand Larry held out, she pulled herself to her feet.

CHAPTER FIVE

The afternoon sunlight gleamed off the shiny new paint on Mr. McGuire's soapbox racer. Mr. McGuire, Matt, and Gordo had worked all weekend taking apart the car and putting it back together. In addition to the fresh paint, they'd stripped the rear flanges, added cool new wheels, and redesigned the steering system. The new soapbox racer was sleek and supremely aerodynamic. Now Mr. McGuire and the boys stood atop the hill above the junior high, admiring their handi-work.

Mr. McGuire turned and looked at the paved walkway that wound down the steep hill. School was out, and all around the hill students were lounging in the grass, studying, playing Frisbee, and just hanging out. Nearby a group of cheerleaders shouted and waved their pom-poms in the air, practicing their moves.

"You're right, Gordo," he said. "This is the perfect hill to test the Sam-tastic Ride."

"Hey!" Matt cried. He pushed up his driving goggles and glared at his father from beneath the crash helmet he wore on his head. As the smallest of the three guys, he fit best in the driver's seat and was going to take the racer on its first ride. "I'm the driver. *And* I'm working on getting us endorsements. We're calling it the Monster Matt Machine."

Gordo stepped between them. He had his

own ideas about what the car should be called. "We'll settle this later," he told Matt and Mr. McGuire. He licked his finger and held it up to test the direction of the wind. "Right now we have primo wind conditions. It's now or never for the Gordinator."

"It's too bad your mother refused to be here," Mr. McGuire said to Matt. "I can't believe she didn't want to see this."

Just then, one of the people playing Frisbee nearby made a wide throw. The disk flew through the air toward the soapbox race car team. "Heads up!" the kid called to them.

Mr. McGuire turned and reached up to catch the disk. But as he did, his foot slipped out from under him. Mr. McGuire fell backward—right onto the soapbox racer. Before Matt or Gordo could do anything, the car started to roll!

"Ahhhhhhhhhhhhhh! Guys!" Mr. McGuire

screamed, desperately trying to steer the car. Gordo and Matt chased after him, but the racer gathered speed and soon outdistanced them. Mr. McGuire's long legs flapped on either side of the car as it hurtled down the hill, knocking over garbage cans and plowing toward a group of students who were standing on the walkway, chatting.

"Watch out!" Mr. McGuire yelled. "Watch out!" The students screamed and dodged out of the way, their books and papers flying. The racer bumped down a short flight of cement steps and passed through a gate marked, DO NOT ENTER.

"Ahhhhhhhhhhhhhhh!" Mr. McGuire cried. Two maintenance men were crossing the walkway, carrying a huge plywood board between them—and Mr. McGuire was headed straight for the board! In the nick of time, the men tilted the board and Mr. McGuire zoomed underneath. He breathed a sigh of relief and turned to look behind him at the board he'd narrowly missed hitting.

"Go, Dad!" Matt cheered.

"Uh-oh," said Gordo. Mr. McGuire's wild ride wasn't over yet. The racer was speeding straight toward a squad of cheerleaders!

"Look out! Get out of the way!" Mr. McGuire yelled, waving one arm while he tried to steer the racer with his other hand. But the cheerleaders were so busy practicing they didn't hear him. Mr. McGuire gritted his teeth and prepared for the worst. At the last second, one of the cheerleaders turned and saw him. Pom-poms scattered as the girls shrieked and leaped out of the way.

At the end of the road, the racer crashed into a small wall and stopped. Mr. McGuire, however, kept going. "Ahhhhhhhhhhhhhh!" he screamed as he was launched from the car.

Matt and Gordo, who were chasing after him, stopped and watched in amazement as Mr. McGuire flew through the air. He belly flopped on the soft grass of the football field. Mrs. McGuire came running up behind them. She'd pulled into the parking lot just in time to see the whole thing.

"Honey?" she called to Mr. McGuire.

At the sound of his wife's voice, Mr. McGuire sat up and shook his head. He turned around and looked at her. "Hi, Jo! Glad you could make it!" he called.

"Well, I never would have forgiven myself if I had missed *that.* Are you okay?" she asked.

"Yeah, I'm fine," Mr. McGuire said, adjusting his glasses, which were dangling from one ear.

"That was awesome, Dad!" Matt cried.

Gordo nodded. "I clocked you at forty-five miles an hour."

Mr. McGuire stood up and dusted the grass

off his shirt. "How's the car?" he asked. Mrs. McGuire and the boys shook their heads.

"I'm sorry," Mrs. McGuire told him. "It didn't make it."

Mr. McGuire walked over to inspect the damage. The entire front end of the wooden car had splintered when it hit the cement wall. "Oh, man, my race car!" Mr. McGuire cried. "Smashed to smithereens." He shook his head sadly.

"Aw, honey," Mrs. McGuire said sympathetically. "What do you say I take you all out for some ice cream . . . "

"All right!" said Matt.

"That'd be great, Mrs. McGuire," Gordo said.

Mrs. McGuire's eyes twinkled. ". . . After you clean up the toolshed. And the backyard. Okay?" She turned and headed back to her car.

Mr. McGuire stuck out his lower lip. "I knew there'd be a catch," he said gloomily.

* * *

Meanwhile, on the lunch patio, Lizzie and
Larry were sitting together at a table. Lizzie
fiddled with her napkin, trying to think of the
best way to let Larry down gently.

Larry took a long drink from his soda and
smiled at Lizzie. "Yesterday, I was just
the Tudge," he said happily. "But today I'm *le*
Tudge. I'm a boyfriend."

"Yeah," Lizzie said, gulping. It was now or
never, she decided. She turned and faced
Larry. "You're awesome," she told him. She
took a deep breath. "But I gotta tell you the
truth." Lizzie carefully removed Larry's *Star
Wars* fan club pin from her jacket collar and
placed it in Larry's hand. "I don't really think
that this relationship is working out for me. I
just don't think we have enough chemistry to
go steady, you know?"

Larry froze, staring down at the pin in

his hand. Lizzie held her breath, dreading his response. She was sure he'd be crushed.

But, to her surprise, Larry nodded. "You're right," he said. "We're living a lie. I mean, I need a girlfriend who's into astrophysics and amphibian skeletal systems and rotisserie baseball."

Lizzie grinned. "You're right. And I need a boyfriend who's into . . . stuff."

Maybe i should develop some interests. Then i can join a club and meet a boy there.

Larry looked at her. "You know, I truly mean this: today was the best day of my life. Lizzie McGuire, you are the nicest person that I know." Lizzie felt a lump in her throat.

i never thought i'd say this, but my mother was right. Great boys do come in odd packages.

This time Lizzie took Larry's hand. She looked right into his brown eyes. "Larry Tudgeman," she said. "Out there is someone really special for you."

"Well, coming from my ex, that means a lot," Larry said, smiling. He picked up his drink and sucked the last of it up through the straw, making a big slurping noise. "So," Larry said when he'd finished his soda. "Do you think I have a chance with Miranda?"

Lizzie shook her head and laughed.

**PART
TWO**

CHAPTER ONE

It was four o'clock on a Tuesday afternoon, and Lizzie McGuire was still in bed. Propped up on a pile of fluffy blue pillows, she flipped through a stack of fashion magazines, now and then reaching over to take a sip from the glass of fresh-squeezed orange juice that stood on her bed stand. If it weren't for the headache, sore throat, and bright red stuffy nose, Lizzie thought as she turned another page of her favorite magazine, being sick wouldn't really be so bad. After only one day of relaxing, she was already feeling better.

Just then, the door to Lizzie's room flew open. Her best friends Miranda and Gordo walked in.

"Hey, guys," said Lizzie. "I didn't know you were coming over."

"We missed you at school," Miranda said. "How are you feeling?"

"Much better." Lizzie nodded. "I'll be back at school tomorrow."

"Well, we brought you your homework," Gordo announced. He dropped a pile of heavy books onto the bed next to Lizzie's feet.

Suddenly, i don't feel so good.

Lizzie looked in astonishment at the huge pile of homework. "Gordo, I've only been sick one day. How much did I miss?"

"Well, Mr. Pettus's lab coat caught on fire in science class," Miranda told her.

Lizzie's eyes opened wide. "Is he okay?" she asked.

"Oh, yeah," Gordo assured her. "It was intentional, part of his lab-safety lecture. You know," he added brightly, "that *stop*, *drop*, *and roll* really does work."

Lizzie imagined her science teacher rolling around on the classroom floor to put out his lab coat. She smiled and shook her head. Goofy Mr. Pettus would do just about anything to get his students to pay attention.

"And Mr. Dig was our sub in English," Miranda told her. "Instead of writing our book reports, he had us play twenty questions. We had to guess which books everyone had read."

"Cool!" Lizzie said.

"Yeah," Gordo added, "but you still have to do your book report."

"Oh." Lizzie pouted. "You guys aren't making me feel any better."

Why is it that school's only fun when i'm not there?

Lizzie looked through the pile of books on her bed. "Okay, so that's English and science. What did I miss in social studies?"

Miranda and Gordo exchanged glances. "Well . . ." Miranda said. She paused and fidgeted with the bangles on her wrist. "Mrs. Stebel gave us a kind of cool project.

Everyone in class was paired up and assigned a country."

"We're supposed to do a report and bring in a native dish. It's Mrs. Stebel's potluck United Nations," Gordo explained.

"Oh, cool!" Lizzie exclaimed. "What country are we doing?"

"Well, er, *we're* doing Mexico," Miranda told her. She shrugged her shoulders uncomfortably and looked at Gordo for help.

"So—what are we cooking?" Lizzie asked enthusiastically.

"Uh . . . tamales," Gordo said, looking down at the tops of his sneakers.

Miranda and Gordo were edging toward the door of Lizzie's room as if they were trying to sneak out before she noticed. Lizzie drew her eyebrows together. *Why are my friends acting so weird?* she wondered. Suddenly the truth dawned on her.

"You guys are paired together," Lizzie said slowly, "aren't you?"

Miranda smiled apologetically. "Yeah."

"So who am I paired with?" Lizzie asked.

"Do you want the good news or the bad news first?" Gordo asked.

Lizzie narrowed her eyes suspiciously. "Who am I paired with?"

"Well, the good news is you'll be exploring the wonderful world of Latvia!" Gordo said brightly.

Lizzie glared at him. "*Who* am I paired with?"

"Well . . . uh . . . you see," Miranda hedged. "Kate was absent from school today, too—"

"Kate?!" Lizzie shrieked. "I have to be paired with *Kate*?"

Kate Sanders was Lizzie's best friend in grade school. Emphasis on *was*. Since they'd started junior high, Kate had become the queen bee of the popular clique, and now she acted as if she could hardly remember Lizzie's name. Kate was the last person in the world Lizzie wanted to spend two minutes with, let alone team up with for a whole social studies project. She looked at Miranda and Gordo, hoping that it was a cruel joke, but she could tell by their embarrassed faces that they weren't kidding. Lizzie sighed. In a crisis situation like this, she thought, there was only one thing to do. She put her pillow over her face and screamed.

"Well," Gordo said to Miranda. "She's taking it better than I expected."

CHAPTER TWO

On Wednesday morning, Lizzie shuffled into the kitchen, still wearing her pink flowered pajamas and fluffy blue slippers. She plopped down in a chair at the breakfast table. Her parents and her ten-year-old brother, Matt, looked at her in surprise.

"Hey," said Lizzie's mother. "I thought you were going to school today."

Lizzie sniffled dramatically and pretended to cough. "No," she croaked. "I'm feeling worse."

Matt eyed her skeptically. "What a coincidence," he said. "You're looking worse, too. But I don't think that has anything to do with being sick." He stuffed another spoonful of cereal in his mouth and chewed loudly.

Lizzie rolled her eyes. "I should've stayed in bed. I'm going back upstairs."

"Your mistake was coming downstairs," Matt told Lizzie in a phony stage whisper, loud enough for their parents to hear. "The key is to stay in bed until they come get you." He shook his head and sighed. "Amateur."

As Lizzie stood up to go back to her room, her mother said, "This doesn't have anything to do with a certain social studies project where you have to work with Kate Sanders, does it?"

"No . . ." Lizzie started to lie, then changed her mind. "Well, yes." She sat back down. "How did you know?"

"I'm a mom," Mrs. McGuire said with a grin. "We have our ways."

"Mrs. Sanders called last night," Mr. McGuire explained.

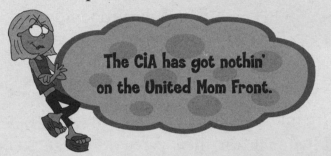

The CiA has got nothin' on the United Mom Front.

"This is so unfair!" Lizzie wailed. "I miss one day of school, and Gordo and Miranda don't cover for me, so now I'm being punished by having to work with Kate."

"You know, sweetie, if you have this much energy at home, you're probably well enough to go to school," Mr. McGuire said.

Lizzie turned to her mother for help. "Mo-om!" she cried.

Mrs. McGuire shook her head. "You and

Kate are going to have to put your differences aside and work together," she said.

Lizzie sighed. "That's impossible."

You don't work with Kate. You work *for* her.

Mrs. McGuire tried again. "You used to be friends—you must have *something* in common."

"Yeah," Lizzie said dryly. "We can't stand each other."

Mrs. McGuire frowned. "Go upstairs and put your clothes on, Lizzie. You're going to be late for school."

Lizzie sighed and stood up from the table. She could tell from her mother's tone that there was no point in arguing this time.

Matt smirked. "You're gonna have a really bad day," he told his sister cheerfully.

Lizzie glared at her brother. "And your day is gonna be *over* if you don't shut your mouth," she snapped. She turned on her heel and stomped out of the room.

Matt was wrong, Lizzie thought later that morning as she headed for her locker after the fourth period bell. She wouldn't call this a really bad day—she'd call it one of the worst days of her entire life! Even though she'd hurried to get ready that morning, she'd been late for school after all, and when she tried to sneak quietly into her first period class, her teacher interrupted his lecture to say, "Thank you for joining us, Ms. McGuire." Of course, the whole class had turned around to look at her. Then, right before science class, the zipper on her backpack broke and all her books had spilled onto the hallway floor—right in front of Ethan Craft! But, worst of all, she knew that she was stuck spending the next two days making Latvian food with Kate Sanders, and Lizzie had just made a not-so-pleasant discovery about Latvian cooking.

Gordo and Miranda were standing at their lockers, when Lizzie arrived.

"This project reeks!" she complained as she fiddled with the combination on her locker. "Not only do I have to work with Kate, but come to find out, Latvia is the food capital of *jellied meat*." She wrinkled her nose in disgust. "This day couldn't get any worse."

Miranda and Gordo looked guiltily at each other. "Well, it's about to," Gordo told Lizzie. He pointed over her shoulder. "Hurricane Kate is here."

Lizzie turned around and saw Kate walking down the hallway, surrounded by a group of popular girls. Kate's long blond hair bounced as though she were in a shampoo commercial as she strode toward Lizzie, but her eyes were narrowed into little slits.

Kate and her posse came to a stop right in front of Lizzie's locker.

Lizzie half-smiled in a way she hoped would seem friendly. "Look, I know we have to work together—" she started.

But Kate lifted her hand and cut her off. "This is the way it's going to work," she snapped. "I spend as little time with you as necessary, we don't work in public, and I am *so* not making jellied meat."

So much for being friendly, Lizzie thought. "Fine," she snapped back. "Why don't you meet me at my house after school?"

"That sounds good," Kate said. She glanced at her friends and added, "I can't possibly run into anyone popular there." The other girls laughed.

Lizzie's cheeks burned, but she wasn't about to let Kate have the last word. She looked her former friend in the eye and said, "But you *do* remember where my house is, right?"

Kate stopped laughing. "I'll see you after school," she said with a sneer. She turned and flounced down the hallway with the other girls trailing after her.

Lizzie slumped against her locker and clutched her head. "I cannot believe I have to work with her," she said miserably.

"Well, that wasn't so bad," Miranda said, trying to sound perky.

"I think you handled it well," Gordo agreed.

"Yeah!" Lizzie exclaimed. "Because I didn't have any help from you guys!"

"It's no big deal," Gordo told her. "All you have to do is give a report and make some food."

Lizzie looked at him in disbelief.

Easy for him to say.
He doesn't have to cook
with Kate-zilla.

Miranda patted Lizzie's shoulder. "It'll be okay," she said.

Lizzie frowned at Miranda. Then she calmly turned, opened her locker, stuck her head inside, and screamed.

Miranda winced. "At least, I *think* it will be okay," she whispered.

Meanwhile, over at Hillridge Elementary School, Matt and his friend Oscar were sitting at a table in the cafeteria, hunched over their lunch trays. While Oscar used his fork to dissect a suspicious-looking piece of lunchroom lasagna, Matt took a bite from his turkey sandwich and chewed thoughtfully.

"You know," Matt said to his friend. "I had the weirdest dream last night. I dreamed that Mrs. McGee was out sick and we didn't have to take our math test."

Oscar looked up from his lunch in surprise. "Matt? Mrs. McGee *is* out sick today and we *don't* have to take our math test."

Matt frowned. "That's weird."

Oscar nodded. "Definitely weird."

Matt took another bite from his sandwich and washed it down with a swig of milk. "But the weirdest part of the dream," he went on, "was that the substitute wore these big red shoes. Like . . . like *clown* shoes."

Suddenly, Oscar turned pale and grabbed Matt's shoulder. He pointed across the cafeteria with his other hand. A tall, unfamiliar teacher was standing next to the lunch counter. And on the teacher's feet was the biggest pair of *bright red shoes* Matt or Oscar had ever seen!

Matt's jaw dropped and his eyes grew wide. He turned to Oscar, "Do you know what this means?" he asked in a hoarse whisper.

Oscar looked at his friend in awe. "That our substitute can get us free tickets to the circus?" he answered hopefully.

"No," Matt said. He thought for a second. "Well, maybe. I don't know." He paused and leaned closer to Oscar. "What I do know is . . . I can predict the future!" He turned to face the lunchroom and raised his fists in the air. "I'm psychic!"

CHAPTER THREE

After school, Lizzie sat in her room, talking to Miranda on the phone, while she waited for Kate to come over.

"Is Kate there yet?" Miranda asked.

"Obviously not," Lizzie replied. "I'm still in one piece." She paced back and forth in front of her bed. "So what are you and Gordo doing?" she asked.

"Oh, we're just doing research," Miranda said, bouncing up and down on her bed.

"*I'm* doing research," Gordo said loudly from Miranda's desk, where he was looking through a pile of books on Mexico. "*You're* talking on the phone." He picked up a pillow and threw it at Miranda.

"Hey!" Miranda laughed. She grabbed the pillow and threw it back at Gordo. He ducked and the pillow hit the books on the desk, knocking them to the floor with a loud *thump*. Miranda and Gordo giggled.

Lizzie listened to her friends' laughter. "Sounds like you guys are having fun," she said miserably.

Miranda waved at Gordo, motioning him to be quiet. "No, no," she told Lizzie somberly. "We're not having fun."

"Right!" Gordo shouted in the background. "There's no fun to be had here." He made a face and threw another pillow at Miranda. They both dissolved into giggles.

Just then, Lizzie heard the doorbell ring. Lizzie groaned. "That's probably Kate. I gotta go," she told Miranda.

"Why? Are you a member of her posse now?" Miranda joked.

"No," Lizzie said, annoyed. "But she *is* my partner on this project, thanks to you guys."

"Sorry," Miranda said.

"Sure you are," Lizzie snapped.

Miranda sighed. "Lizzie, what do you want me to do?"

i want you to build a time machine, go back to yesterday's class, and when Mrs. Stebel asks who wants to be Lizzie's partner, RAISE YOUR HAND!

"There's nothing you can do. I'll see you tomorrow," she told Miranda, and then added, "if I survive." Lizzie hung up the phone, shaking her head. She took a deep breath and headed downstairs.

In the kitchen, Kate was leaning against the counter, talking to Lizzie's mom. Lizzie stood in the doorway for a moment, watching them.

"Kate, we haven't seen you around here in so long," Lizzie's mom said.

"It really has been much too long, Mrs. McGuire," Kate agreed in a syrupy voice.

"So, what have you been up to?" Mrs. McGuire asked, obviously trying to make conversation.

"Oh, I've been *really* busy," Kate said in the same phony tone. Lizzie wanted to barf.

Lizzie couldn't stand listening to Kate's fake friendliness a minute longer. She walked into the kitchen.

"Oh, there she is!" Mrs. McGuire said with relief. "I know you two have a lot of work to do, so I'll let you get right to it." She patted Lizzie's shoulder and hurried off to another part of the house.

Lizzie stared at Kate. Kate folded her arms and stared back at Lizzie. Lizzie's eyes narrowed. The room was so quiet, they could have heard a flea sneeze.

"Look," Lizzie said at last. "I don't want to work with you any more than you want to work with me, okay?"

Kate snorted. "Doubt it."

That's it! The gloves are coming off!

Lizzie had known this wouldn't be fun, but Kate was making it a hundred times worse. "You know, you weren't my first choice, either," Lizzie exclaimed, stalking back and forth in front of the kitchen counter. "The only reason I got *stuck* with you is because I was sick and my friends weren't looking out for me."

"You think *your* friends are bad?" Kate snapped. "I was sick, and Claire picked Ethan over me. So now I'm stuck with you."

"I hate my friends," both girls said at the same time. They looked at each other and laughed in surprise.

Did we just agree on something? That's scary.

But almost as soon as they'd started, the

girls stopped laughing and looked away from each other uncomfortably. After all, this wasn't supposed to be fun. Kate ran her hand through her hair and frowned. Lizzie folded her arms and looked awkwardly at the floor.

"We'd better get to work," she said at last.

"Step right up! Step right up! Have your fortune told by the Amazing Matt!" Oscar shouted, cupping his hands around his mouth to form a makeshift megaphone. "Don't miss this chance to have the neighborhood's only ten-year-old psychic tell your future!"

As Oscar shouted, he circled the McGuires' backyard like a ringmaster at a circus, calling more kids in from the street. Already a long line stretched from the McGuires' backyard around to the front of their house. Everyone wanted to see if Matt McGuire really could predict the future.

Matt sat in a folding chair in the backyard, calmly surveying the crowd, his hands clasped together on a card table in front of him. He was wearing a bright orange bedsheet around his shoulders like a cloak, and his spiky brown hair was covered by a gold embroidered turban with a crooked ostrich feather sticking out the front. A sign written in glittery gold letters hung from the edge of the table:

THE AMAZING MATT
FORTUNES TOLD—25 CENTS

"Bring in the next group!" Matt called.

Oscar hurried to the head of the line and ushered three kids over to Matt's booth. The first kid, a boy wearing a huge blue backpack, stepped forward and placed his quarter on the table. Matt took the quarter, dropped it in a jam jar near his feet, then looked closely at the

boy, bringing his fingers to his turbaned forehead in concentration.

"Save your money," he advised. "I predict
you will be buying an expensive gift."

The boy frowned. *This* was the fortune he'd
paid twenty-five cents for?

Matt turned to the girl standing next to the
boy with the backpack. She had long, sandy
brown hair with shaggy bangs that flopped
over her eyes. She placed her quarter in Matt's
outstretched hand.

"I see a haircut in your immediate future,"
Matt told her. The girl rolled her eyes.

The third kid, a tall boy chewing a huge
wad of bubble gum, reluctantly gave Matt his
money. He folded his arms and blew a giant
bubble, looking at Matt skeptically over the
top of the rubbery pink gum.

"I see you going on a long, long trip," Matt
said. The tall boy scowled and his bubble

popped. "Man, this is a rip-off," he complained. The longhaired girl and the boy with the blue backpack nodded in agreement. Together they started to walk away, when suddenly . . .

The tall boy tripped over a lawn ornament. *Phooottt*—his gum flew out of his mouth. The pink glob flew through the air and landed right in the long brown hair of the girl standing next to him! The girl shrieked and flailed her arms, trying to get rid of the gum. In her confusion, she knocked into the boy holding the blue backpack, sending the boy sprawling onto the lawn, while his bag launched into the air. It flew toward the McGuires' house . . . and smashed through the living room window. The kids gasped.

A second later, Matt's dad came out of the house. He held up the blue backpack and looked around at the group of kids clustered on the lawn. "Whoever owns this backpack is paying for a new window!" he declared angrily.

A hush fell over the crowd. Everyone's jaw dropped in amazement. They gaped at Matt.

Matt smiled, leaned back in his chair, and put his hands behind his head. "What can I say?" he told them. "I'm the real deal."

Meanwhile, Lizzie and Kate were sitting in the McGuires' kitchen, surrounded by books on Latvia. They were still trying to come up with a Latvian recipe that seemed vaguely . . . edible.

Lizzie glanced through a cookbook. "We could make . . . gray peas and fried meat."

"What's in that?" Kate asked.

Lizzie looked at her. "Gray peas and fried meat."

"Ugh." Kate stuck out her tongue. "I don't even like *green* peas."

"Why couldn't we get France?" Lizzie complained. "All we'd have to do is go buy some bread. And sparkling juice."

Kate smiled. "And fries," she added. The two girls laughed.

Just then, Lizzie's mom walked into the kitchen. "You guys seem like you're having fun," she remarked, looking at their smiling faces.

"I don't know if 'fun' is the word," Kate said dryly.

"Just wait until tomorrow when we actually have to cook something Latvian," Lizzie said. The idea was so ridiculous that she and Kate started laughing again.

"Wow." Mrs. McGuire smiled. "This is like old times."

Lizzie and Kate stopped laughing and looked at each other. Lizzie's mom was right. It was just like old times, back when they were friends. Except for one tiny fact: they weren't friends anymore. Not by a long shot.

The room filled with an awkward silence.

"I didn't realize it was so late. I gotta motor," Kate said quickly, gathering up her books. "Can't be late for cheerleading practice."

"Yeah, you'd better go," Lizzie said flatly.

Kate hesitated. "Well, bye," she said, and turned away.

"See you tomorrow," Lizzie told her, not getting up from her chair. Mrs. McGuire and Lizzie watched Kate leave. Then Mrs. McGuire turned to her daughter.

"What was that?" she asked.

"What was what?" said Lizzie.

"Well, when I walked in here, you guys looked like you were getting along. Like when you used to be friends," Mrs. McGuire said.

"We weren't getting along," Lizzie corrected her. "We were just studying."

Mrs. McGuire smiled knowingly. "Oh, okay," she said. "Sure you were."

CHAPTER FOUR

"**S**he lives!" Gordo declared the next morning when he and Miranda saw Lizzie standing at her locker.

Lizzie turned and grinned at them. "Hey, guys," she said.

Miranda patted her friend's shoulder consolingly. "I knew you'd make it."

"How'd it go?" Gordo asked.

Lizzie paused. What should she tell them?

it was the most horrible experience of my life.

"It wasn't terrible," she admitted finally.

"Wow," Gordo said. "Good attitude."

"Yeah," Miranda added, "but we're sorry for sticking you with Kate. We should've been looking out for you."

Gordo looked at Miranda in horror. "I didn't want to work with Kate!" he blurted out. Miranda punched him in the arm. "Ow," said Gordo. He shot Miranda a look, then turned back to Lizzie. "Anyway, I bet Kate makes you do all the research. Right?"

Lizzie shook her head. "No, she doesn't."

"Just wait until you start cooking," said Miranda. "She'll be too worried about breaking a nail to do anything."

Lizzie smiled. "I think it'll be okay," she said.

"Well, we're going to be doing our work at the Digital Bean after school if you want some Kate-free time," Gordo told Lizzie. The gang often met at the Digital Bean, a nearby cybercafé, to surf the net and chill.

"Actually, Kate and I are meeting at the Digital Bean to finish our project," she said.

Miranda and Gordo looked at her in surprise. "Wait. I thought she didn't want to be seen with you in public," Miranda reminded her.

Lizzie made a face. "It's not like I want to hang out with her, either. But the Digital Bean has DSL." Lizzie explained how the night before it had taken her forty-five minutes to download a site from Latvia. "Come to find out, it was a fan club for an Eastern European supermodel." Gordo and Miranda laughed.

The three friends agreed to see one another

later at the Digital Bean and headed off to class.

Later that afternoon, Lizzie and Kate sat together, looking at a computer screen in the Digital Bean café. Lizzie typed "Latvia recipes" into a search engine, then clicked through the resulting Web sites.

"I'll be so glad when this project is over tomorrow," Kate muttered, watching Lizzie scroll through a list of recipes. "So what're we making?"

"We can make . . . '*sult*,'" Lizzie suggested. "It's only four letters. How hard could it be?"

"What's in it?" Kate asked.

Lizzie double-clicked on the recipe and read the ingredients: "Veal and jelly."

"Ewwwwww!" the girls cried together.

Lizzie skimmed through a few more recipes. "I cannot believe how quick this connection is!" she exclaimed.

"Wait, go back!" Kate cried suddenly, pointing at the screen. Lizzie clicked back to the previous recipe. The graphic showed a picture of a layered pastry covered in powered sugar. "Aleksander Torte," Kate read. She raised her eyebrows. "That doesn't look too bad."

Lizzie looked at the recipe. "We can pronounce it, and it doesn't involve any jellied meat."

Kate laughed. "Coolie!" She raised her hand for a high five.

Lizzie laughed too and slapped Kate's hand.

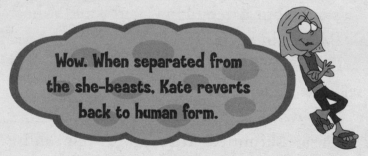

Wow. When separated from the she-beasts, Kate reverts back to human form.

Just then, Miranda and Gordo approached their table.

"Hey, Lizzie," Miranda said, then pretended to do a double take when she saw Kate. "Who's your new friend?" she asked sarcastically.

"Don't worry," Gordo told Kate in an exaggerated whisper. "We won't call attention to the fact that you two are out together *in public.*"

Kate rolled her eyes. Embarrassed, Lizzie tried to smile. "Come on, you guys. We're trying to study here," she said.

"Let's go, Gordo," Miranda said. "We have to finish making our tamales." She flashed a big, fake smile at Kate, then gave Lizzie a sympathetic look and held her thumb and her ear like a phone, signaling that Lizzie should call her later.

"I can't believe those are your friends," Kate said when they were gone.

Before Lizzie had a chance to answer, Kate's best friend Claire walked over, surrounded by a group of other cheerleaders. Claire glanced at Lizzie and smirked.

"Kate, are we slumming?" she asked. The other girls laughed.

Kate's face flushed with anger and embarrassment. "We're just working on our social studies project," she snapped. "I didn't get to choose my partner, *remember*?"

"Well, Ethan and I are having a *great* time making Chinese food," Claire told her. "Anyway, call me when you climb back up the social ladder. Later." With a flip of her hand, Claire walked away. The other girls followed, tossing their hair. None of them even bothered to say good-bye to Lizzie.

Lizzie looked after them with disgust. "I can't believe those are *your* friends."

Kate looked frustrated for a moment, but she quickly recovered and gave Lizzie a condescending look. "You obviously don't know what it's like to be popular."

> But when backed into a corner,
> she-beasts come out fighting.

"Coming here was a total mistake," Kate added. "Let's just print out that recipe and go before anyone else sees us." Lizzie didn't need to be told twice. Both girls angrily gathered their things and fled the café without another word.

A few blocks away, at the McGuire house, Matt and his parents were sitting together on the couch. While Mrs. McGuire read a book, her husband flipped through the television channels with the remote control.

"News," Matt predicted, just as a news station came onto the TV screen.

"News . . . news . . . news . . . news," Matt said again, each time just before Mr. McGuire landed on another news station.

Mr. McGuire stared at his son. "How do you do that?" he asked.

"Dad, I'm psychic," Matt replied.

"Sam, it's four o'clock," Mrs. McGuire said, without looking up from her book. "There's nothing on TV *but* news. Even *I* could tell you that."

"But you're not psychic," Matt said.

Mrs. McGuire looked at him. "And neither are you."

Matt turned to his father. "I knew she was going to say that," Matt informed him.

"Really?" Mr. McGuire said in surprise. "Hey, have you got any idea about tomorrow's lottery numbers?"

Matt crossed his fingers and screwed up his face in concentration. "One . . ." he said. "Two . . ."

Mr. McGuire quickly dug a pen out of his pocket and began to write the numbers down on a scrap of paper.

"Three . . ." Matt said.

Mrs. McGuire shut her book with a snap. "Sam, put the pen down," she commanded. "He is not psychic."

"Am, too," Matt countered.

Mrs. McGuire crossed her arms and fixed him with a stern look. "Okay, tell me what I'm thinking."

"You're thinking . . ." Matt eyed his mother thoughtfully. "You're thinking you're going to send me to my room." Matt and his dad looked eagerly at Mrs. McGuire, waiting to see if he was right.

Mrs. McGuire pursed her lips. "Lucky

guess. Matt, you are not psychic. I'm predictable."

Matt stood up to leave. "Say what you will, but being psychic isn't exactly fun. It's a huge responsibility, knowing what the future holds." He grinned at his parents and went off to his room.

"You know, he's right," Mr. McGuire said seriously. "That is a huge responsibility."

Mrs. McGuire gaped at him in amazement. "Sam, he is not psychic," she insisted. "He can't read minds or predict the future. Stop encouraging him."

"Don't believe her, Dad!" Matt yelled from his room at the other end of the house.

Mr. McGuire raised his eyebrows and looked at his wife. "Now, *that* was spooky," he said.

Mrs. McGuire frowned at him. "It wasn't spooky—it was coincidence." They stared at each other for a moment. Mrs. McGuire could tell he still agreed with Matt. "Okay," she said, putting her hands on her hips. "I am going to prove to both of you that he's not psychic."

"Am, too!" Matt called.

A short time later, Matt was again sitting on the living room couch, this time blindfolded with a red handkerchief that Mrs. McGuire had tied over his eyes. His parents stood on the carpet in front of him.

"Mom, Dad, I'm psychic. Why can't you just be supportive?" Matt complained.

"I *am* supportive," Mr. McGuire said.

Mrs. McGuire shot her husband a look. Then she leaned down so her face was even with Matt's. "I'm supportive, too, honey," she told him in a kind voice, then added, "but you're not psychic."

"But everything I say comes true," said Matt.

"Honey, it's just a coincidence. And I'm going to prove to you that you're not psychic. To both of you," she added.

Mr. McGuire waved his hand in front of Matt's face. "Can you see anything?" he asked.

"Uh, no, Dad," Matt replied patiently. "I'm blindfolded."

Mrs. McGuire looked at her husband and nodded. Mr. McGuire held up three fingers.

"How many fingers is your father holding up?" Mrs. McGuire asked.

"Three," Matt promptly answered.

Matt's parents were silent for a moment, studying Mr. McGuire's fingers.

"I'm right, aren't I?" Matt asked.

Mrs. McGuire shook her head at her husband, indicating that he should say "no."

"Yes," Mr. McGuire said, raising his eyebrows at his wife.

Mrs. McGuire flopped down on the couch next to Matt and rested her chin on her hand. She opened her mouth to say something, but Matt cut her off.

"Now, Mom's upset because Dad didn't lie to me and tell me that I got the wrong answer," he said confidently.

"I'm not upset," Mrs. McGuire said angrily.

Mr. McGuire leaned closer to his wife and lowered his voice. "You seem a little upset," he said. Mrs. McGuire scowled.

"I'll be in my room," Matt said, standing up from the couch.

"No, you wait right there," Mrs. McGuire ordered, pointing her finger at his blind-folded face. "I am going to prove to you that you're not psychic. Sit down."

Matt sank back into the sofa cushions. "I knew that was going to happen," he said.

CHAPTER FIVE

Late that afternoon, Lizzie and Kate stood in the McGuires' kitchen. They were working on the Aleksander Torte—but they weren't exactly working together. Lizzie silently measured out several cups of flour and sifted them into a mixing bowl, while Kate gingerly cracked eggs into a separate bowl, her lips clamped together. Neither of them spoke. When Lizzie turned to the refrigerator to get some butter, her shoulder accidentally bumped against Kate's. Kate scowled at her.

"Lizzie," Kate grumbled to herself.

A few moments later, Kate accidentally joggled Lizzie's arm when she went to the refrigerator for more eggs. The flour Lizzie was sifting spilled onto the counter. Lizzie frowned.

"Kate," she muttered impatiently.

"Let's just get this over with!" Kate said.

"Fine with me," Lizzie said. "We'll make the torte, and it will be over." She grabbed the flour bag and started to march to the fridge. "Watch out—coming through!"

"Careful!" Still holding the carton of eggs, Kate stepped back as a puff of flour flew from the top of the bag.

"Sorry," Lizzie said. She put the bag back down on the counter.

Kate cautiously looked down at the diamond-patterned dress she was wearing, checking to make sure that no flour had got onto it. "Tell me why I wore something new to bake in?" she said to no one in particular.

"Because you always do," Lizzie replied.

Kate stared at her. "What are you talking about?" she demanded.

"Do you remember your ninth birthday party?" Lizzie asked.

Kate thought a minute. "I had a sleepover," she said. "You and Miranda were there."

"Yeah. And you got that Baby Spice shirt you wanted so bad," Lizzie reminded her.

Kate nodded slowly. "And I had to put it on right away. . . ."

"After your mom told you not to," Lizzie added.

"Because we were baking cookies." Kate smiled at the memory.

Lizzie laughed, thinking about the cookie-dough disaster in the Sanderses' kitchen. "We made a total mess," she said.

Kate nodded and laughed, too. "My mom had to wash that shirt four times before the egg finally came out. That was my all-time favorite shirt." She thought for a moment, then asked, "Who gave that to me?"

Lizzie hesitated, then looked carefully at Kate. "I did," she said.

Before Kate could reply, Matt suddenly came charging into the kitchen, still blindfolded and waving his arms.

"I'm psychic!" he cried triumphantly. "I can see all!"

Wham! Matt ran smack into Kate, sending

the carton of eggs she was holding flying into the air.

"Look out!" Lizzie cried, pushing Kate out of the way as the eggs splattered on the floor. Lizzie glared at her younger brother. "Matt!" she groaned.

Kate looked down at the puddles of egg slime on the floor. "Eww," she said.

Matt pulled off his blindfold and looked around the messy kitchen in confusion. "I . . . I didn't see that coming," he said. He turned to his parents, who had just entered the room and were watching him with a mixture of annoyance and amusement. Matt squinted and looked closely at his mother's face. "I don't know what you're thinking," he said, clearly astonished.

"Really?" Mr. McGuire said dryly.

"Because you *should*," Mrs. McGuire added, cocking an eyebrow.

"I think I've lost the gift," Matt declared. "I'll be in my room." Hanging his head, Matt shuffled away.

Mr. McGuire watched him leave; then he turned to his wife. "Wow," he said. "He really isn't psychic anymore." Mrs. McGuire rolled her eyes.

"Do you girls need any help cleaning this mess up?" she asked.

"No, it's okay," Lizzie answered. "It's just a few eggs."

"We've got it under control," Kate assured Lizzie's mom.

"Okay," Mrs. McGuire said. She looked at her husband. "Let's go talk to Matt."

"Do you think he knows we're coming?" Mr. McGuire asked. Mrs. McGuire gave the back of her husband's head a playful swat as the two headed off toward their son's room.

After her parents were gone, Lizzie turned to

Kate. "How's your outfit? Any egg?" she asked.

Kate looked down and carefully inspected her dress. "Nope, egg free." She grinned at Lizzie and held up her hand for a high five.

Lizzie smiled and stepped forward to slap Kate's hand. But—*whoops*—just as she touched Kate's hand, Lizzie skidded on the slippery floor. She reached out an arm to steady herself, but instead knocked over the bag of flour. The two girls tumbled into a heap on the floor, and the flour landed on top of them, coating them both in white powder.

Kate's eyes grew wide as she looked down at her new dress, which was now covered in flour *and* egg goo. Lizzie held her breath, waiting for Kate to explode. . . .

But suddenly Kate began to giggle. Then she started to laugh. Lizzie sighed with relief and laughed, too. In a moment both girls were laughing so hard they could barely speak.

"Um, Kate, I hate to break it to you, but you're no longer egg free," Lizzie gasped.

"You should see yourself, McGuire," Kate said, pointing to a big smudge of flour on Lizzie's nose.

"Now this is just like your ninth birthday," Lizzie said.

"Yeah," Kate agreed. "But we have to have a sleepover and stay up all night, talking."

Lizzie smiled. "Do you remember when your mom kept coming downstairs and telling us to go to bed?"

"Yeah, that was so much fun." Kate sighed and looked at Lizzie. "What *did* we talk about?"

"Everything. School. Boys." Lizzie glanced at Kate, then added, "And how we'd always be friends."

Both girls were silent for a moment. "What happened?" Kate asked softly.

Lizzie shook her head. "I don't know."

i know! She got popular.

"One summer you went off to camp and when you came back . . ." Lizzie paused. "Well . . . everything was different."

Kate nodded, remembering. "I guess that it was."

"And then we just weren't friends anymore," Lizzie added.

Kate looked down for a second. "It's weird how that happens," she said.

"Yeah, it is," said Lizzie.

"It seems kind of dumb," Kate said, looking hesitantly back at Lizzie.

Lizzie smiled sadly. "Yeah," she agreed. "It does."

On Friday afternoon, Kate and Lizzie stood in front of Mrs. Stebel's social studies class, giving their presentation. Between them they held up a colorful poster board collage of information on Latvia.

"Latvia has, like, been controlled by many other countries," Kate told the class, pointing out the tiny country on a map of Eastern Europe.

"But it became independent in August of 1991," Lizzie added

"The country's cuisine has been heavily influenced by Russia," Kate said, this time pointing out nearby Russia on the map.

"So there's a lot of overlap in traditional Eastern European foods," Lizzie explained, deciding not to mention the jellied meat.

"We made Aleksander Torte." Kate put down her end of the poster and lifted up the

raspberry-filled pastry she and Lizzie had prepared the day before. The two girls glanced at
each other and smiled.

"So, if anyone's brave enough, come and
try a piece," Lizzie announced.

The other students in the class stood up
from their seats and hurried forward to try a
piece of the delicious-looking cake. Kate
and Lizzie each picked up a slice and took a
bite.

"Hey!" Kate said with surprise. "This is so
not bad!"

Lizzie nodded and wiped the powdered
sugar off her lips with a paper napkin. "We
made a pretty good team," she said.

Kate smiled. "Yeah," she agreed. "We did."

Just then, Claire and the other cheerleaders
walked up to Kate. At the same moment, Gordo
and Miranda came over to stand next to Lizzie.

Miranda looked Kate's friends up and

down. "So, Claire? Do you miss having someone bossing you around?" she asked. Lizzie winced.

Claire glanced at Miranda as if she were a squashed bug, then turned to Kate. "Are you done hanging out in Dorktown?" she asked. "Because I think 'loser' is contagious." Kate's eyebrows drew together in a pained expression.

Gordo took a step closer to Claire. "You couldn't even *spell* contagious," he told her. Lizzie and Kate both flinched unhappily, listening to their friends insult one another.

"Well?" Claire said, placing her hands on her hips and looking at Kate.

"Well?" Gordo and Miranda said, turning to Lizzie.

Lizzie and Kate looked at each other. For a moment, it seemed that maybe they could ignore their cliques and be friends, after all.

But in a split second, the moment passed. Kate's eyes narrowed into little slits. Lizzie glared back at her.

Three strikes, and you're out!

"Nice working with you. *Not.*" Kate sneered at Lizzie.

"Weren't you just leaving?" Lizzie snapped back.

"Geek," said Kate.

"Snob," Lizzie countered.

Kate wrinkled her nose in disgust. Then, with a flip of her hair, she turned and strode toward the door. Claire and the other cheerleaders hurried after her.

Did i really think things were going to change? After all, this *is* junior high.

Gordo put his arm around Lizzie's shoulders. "Did we already apologize for leaving you with Kate?" he asked sympathetically.

Miranda came up on Lizzie's other side. "I couldn't even imagine the pain you had to go through," she said.

Lizzie looked over to the door of the classroom where Kate was standing with her posse. Just then, Kate looked back over her shoulder at Lizzie. The two girls shared a secret smile. Then Lizzie turned back to her friends.

"No," Lizzie agreed quietly. "You probably couldn't."

GET INSIDE HER HEAD
Lizzie McGUIRE
A Disney Channel Original Series
Visit Lizzie @ ZoogDisney.com
©Disney
Weekends on
DISNEY CHANNEL
SM

SHE CAN DO ANYTHING.

COMING IN JUNE 2002

ZoogDisney.com

©Disney

Disney
CHANNEL ℠